HEY, DIDDLE DIDDLE

DIDDLE

KIN EAGLE

ILLUSTRATED BY ROB GILBERT

Gareth Stevens Publishing
MILWAUKEE

For a free color catalog describing Gareth Stevens' list
of high-quality books and multimedia programs, call
1-800-542-2595 (USA) or 1-800-461-9120 (Canada).
Gareth Stevens Publishing's Fax: (414) 225-0377.

Library of Congress Cataloging-in-Publication Data

Eagle, Kin.
    Hey, diddle diddle / by Kin Eagle; illustrated by
Rob Gilbert.
        p. cm. — (Extended nursery rhymes)
    Summary: This expanded version of the traditional
rhyme shows what happened after the cow jumped over
the moon. Includes music on the last page.
    ISBN 0-8368-2485-7 (lib. bdg.)
    1. Children's songs—Texts. [1. Cows—Songs and
music. 2. Songs.] I. Gilbert, Roby, 1966- ill. II. Title.
III. Series.
PZ8.3.E112515He   1999
782.42164'0268—dc21
[E]   99-25779

This edition first published in 1999 by
Gareth Stevens Publishing
1555 North RiverCenter Drive, Suite 201
Milwaukee, WI 53212 USA

Text © 1997 by Kin Eagle. Illustrations © 1997 by Rob Gilbert.
Original edition published in 1997 by Whispering Coyote Press,
300 Crescent Court, Suite 860, Dallas, TX 75201.

Printed in the United States of America

1 2 3 4 5 6 7 8 9 03 02 01 00 99

For Sam and Toni,
and for Adam, Jonathan, and Benjamin
—K.E.

For Juliette and Sky,
with all my love
—R.G.

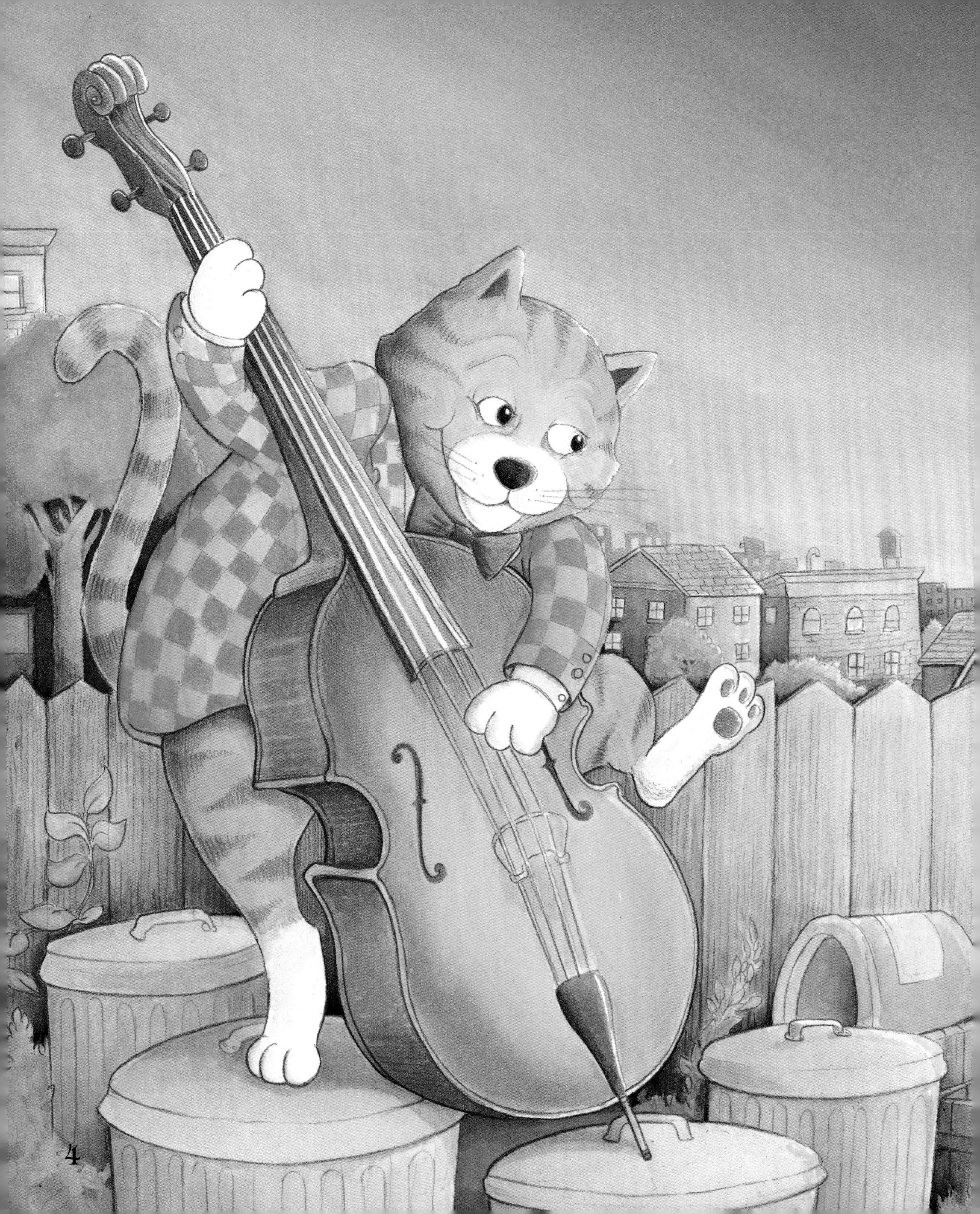

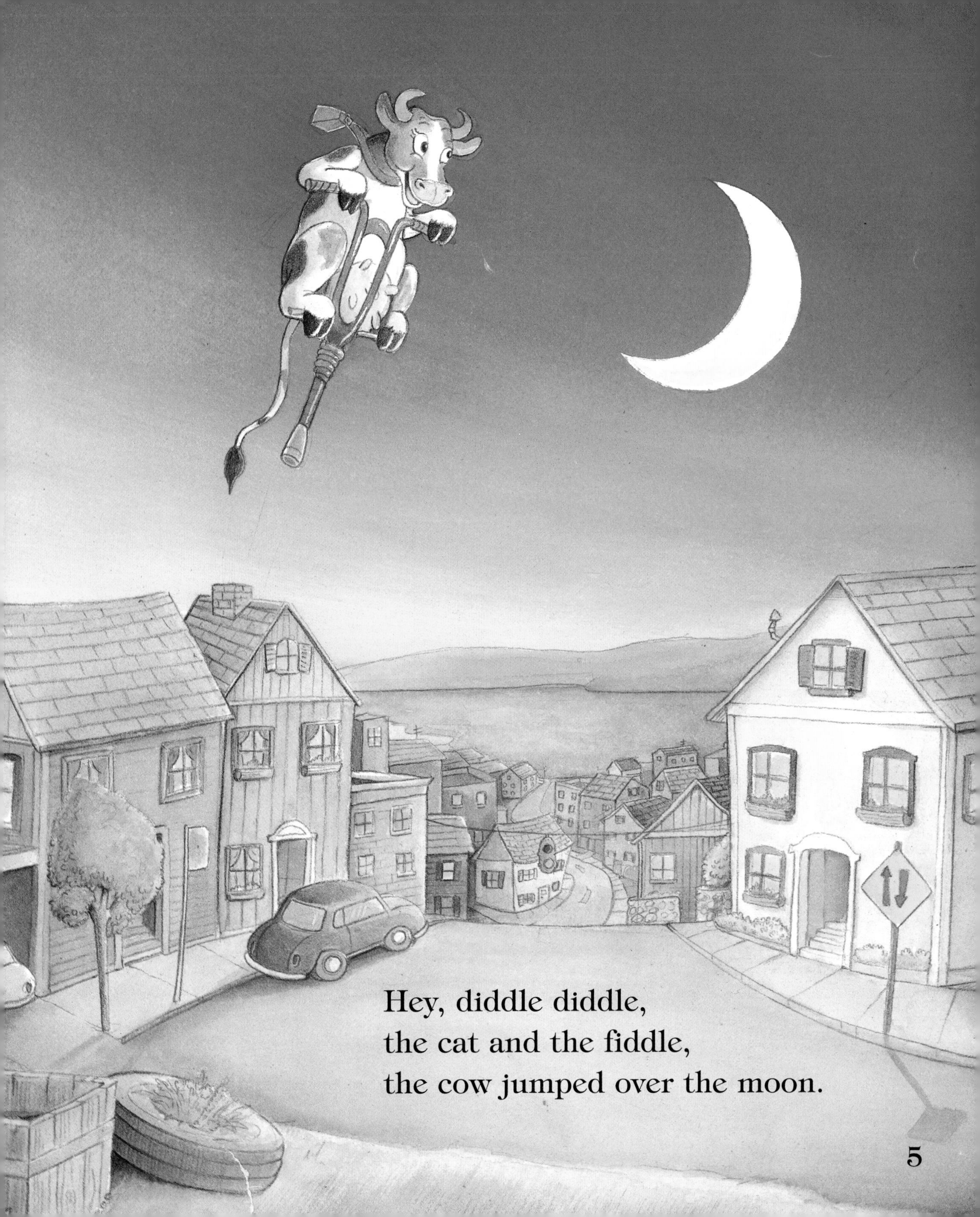

Hey, diddle diddle,
the cat and the fiddle,
the cow jumped over the moon.

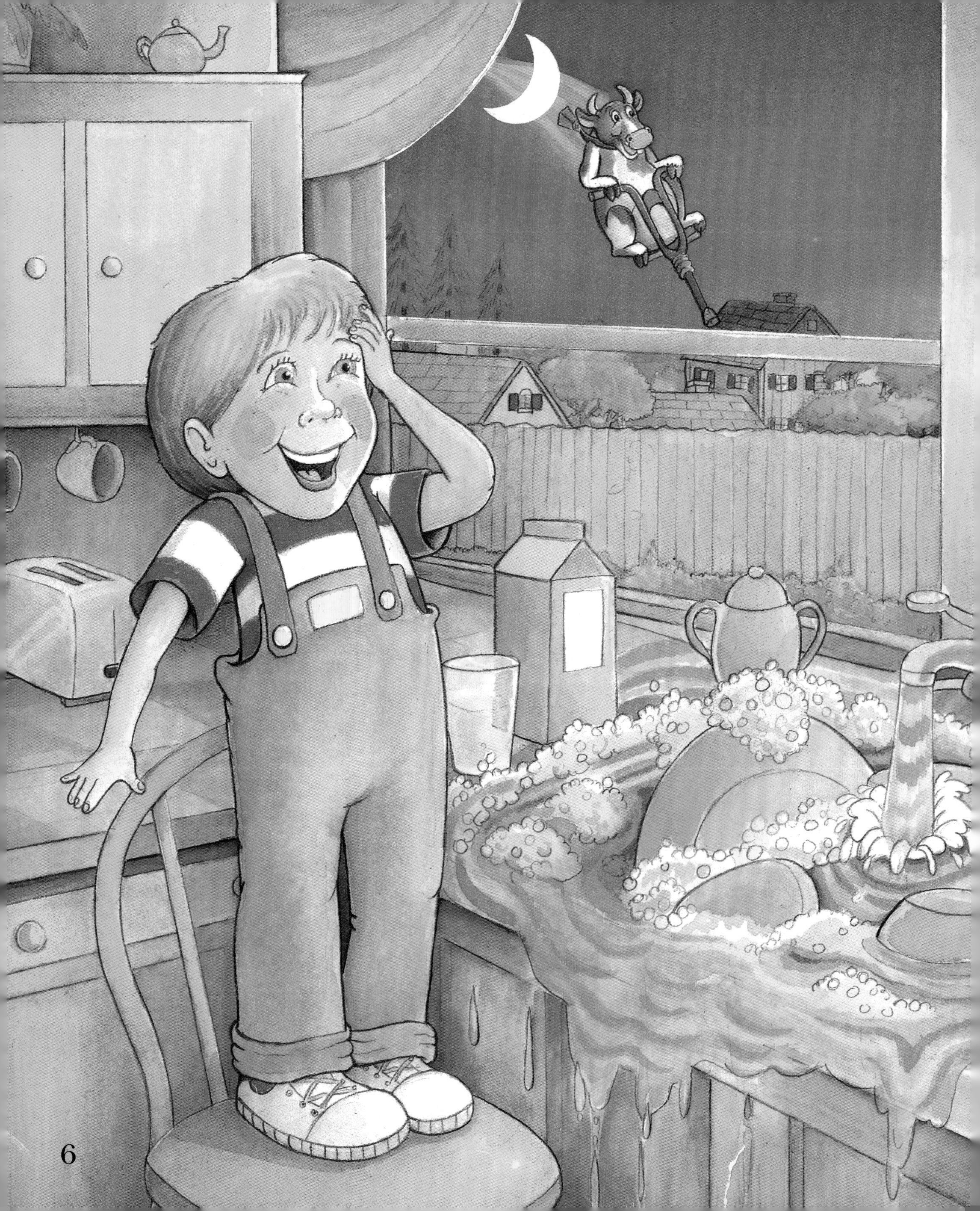

The little boy laughed
to see such a sight
and the dish ran away with the spoon.

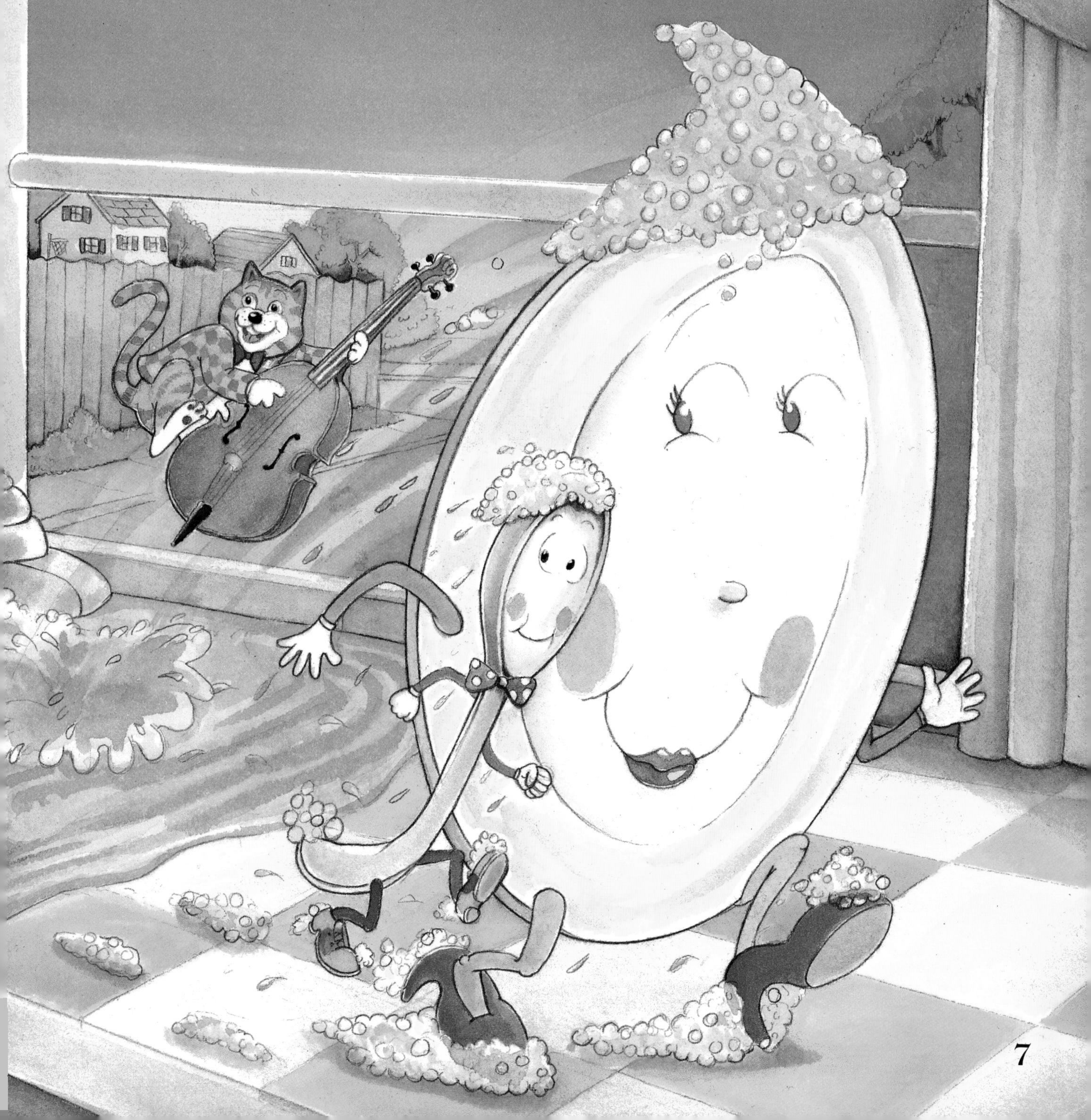

The puss with the fiddle
asked his new friend a riddle:
"What's black, what's white, and brown, too?"
"Don't know," said the cow,
"I give up, tell me now."
And they laughed, "Silly cow, why it's you!"

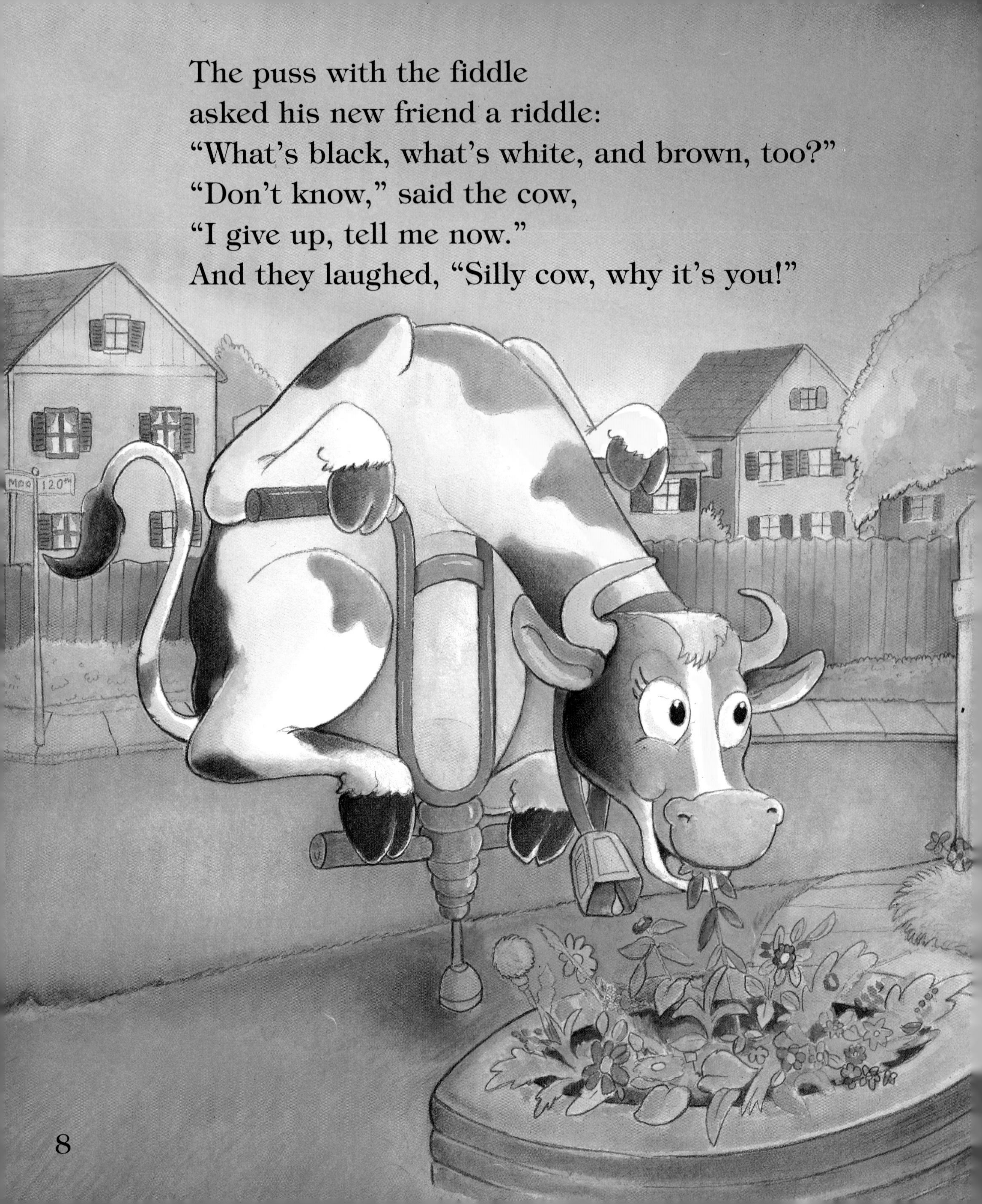
Moo
120th

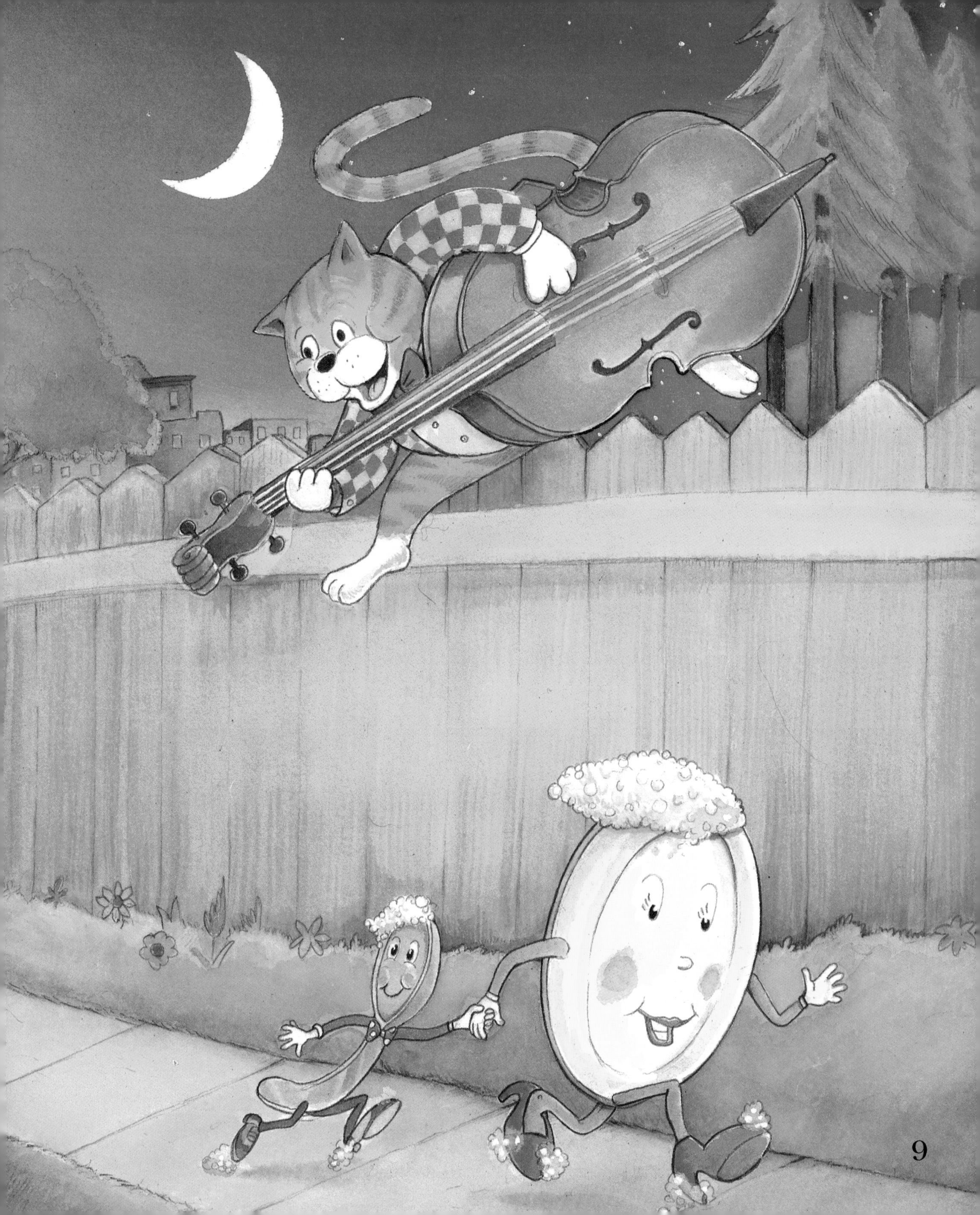

The cow was out grazing
when just then—amazing!—
she suddenly leaped to the moon.

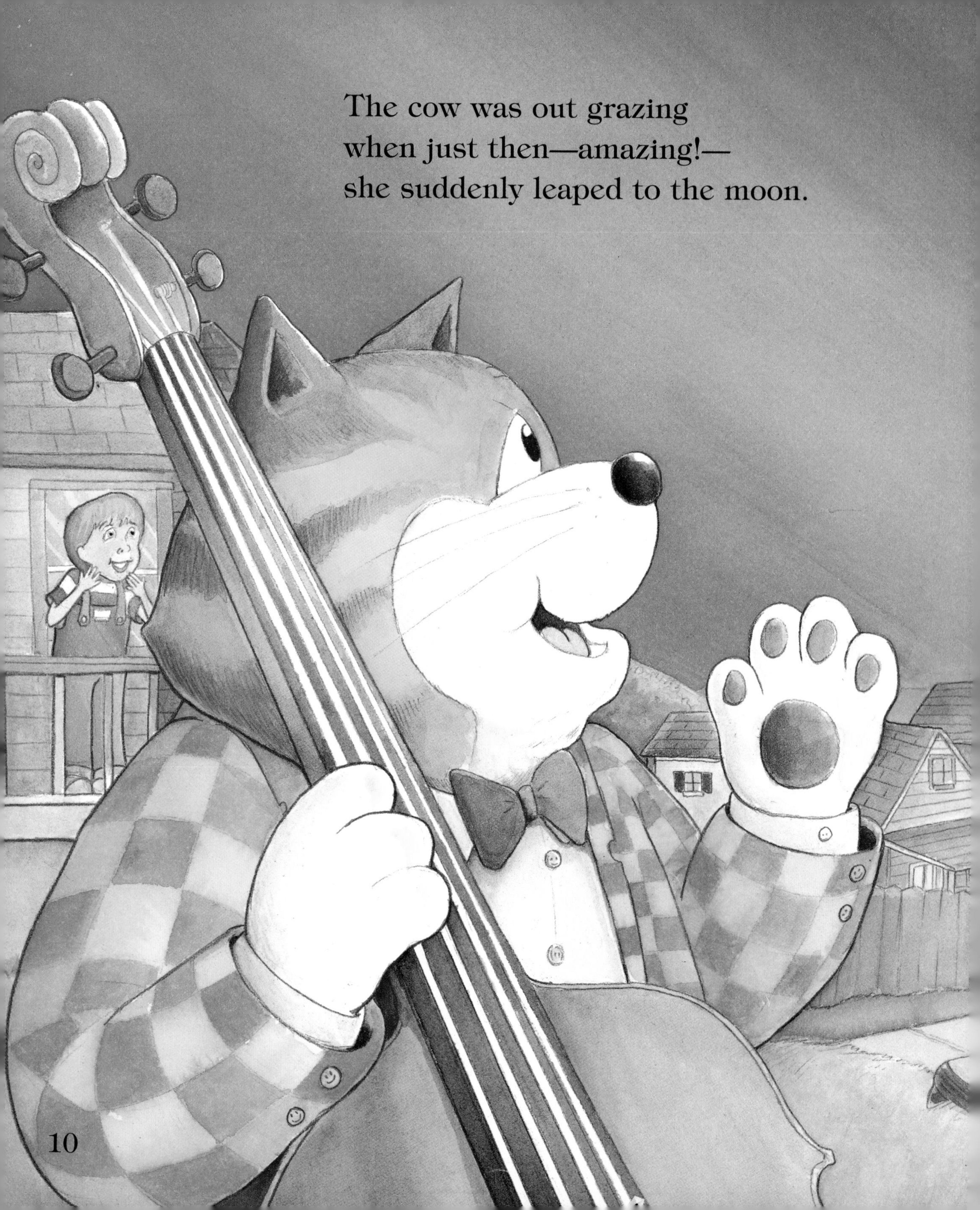

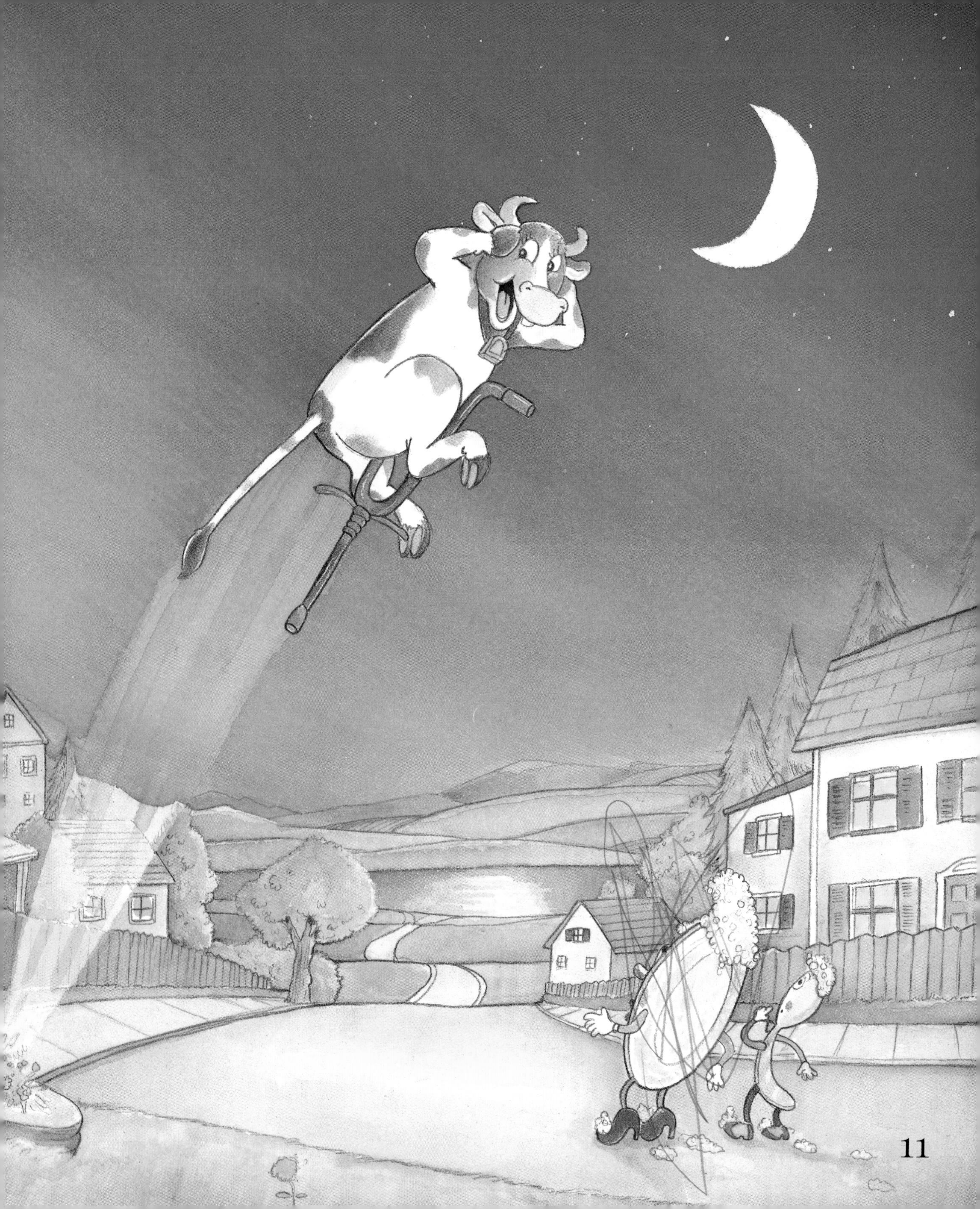

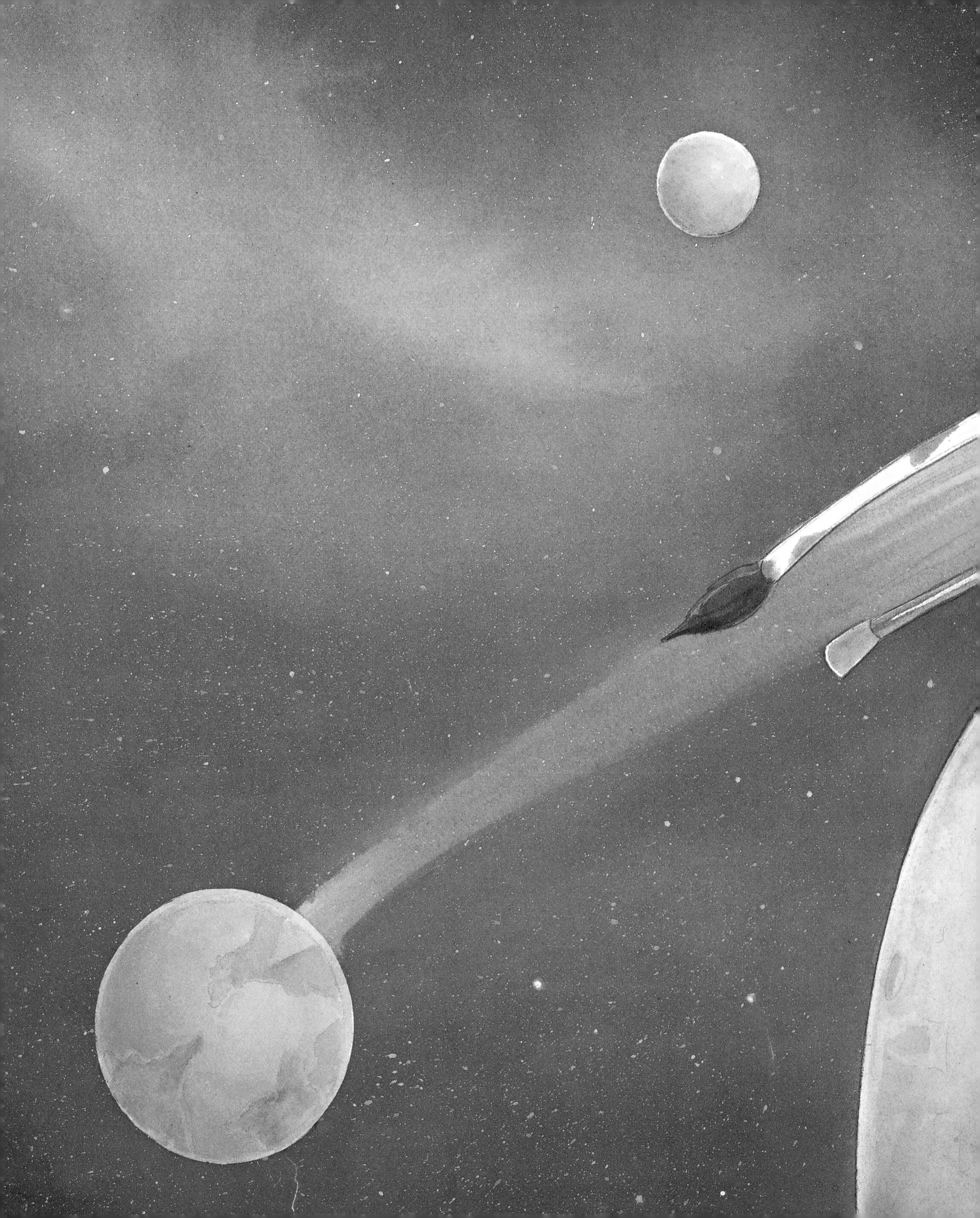

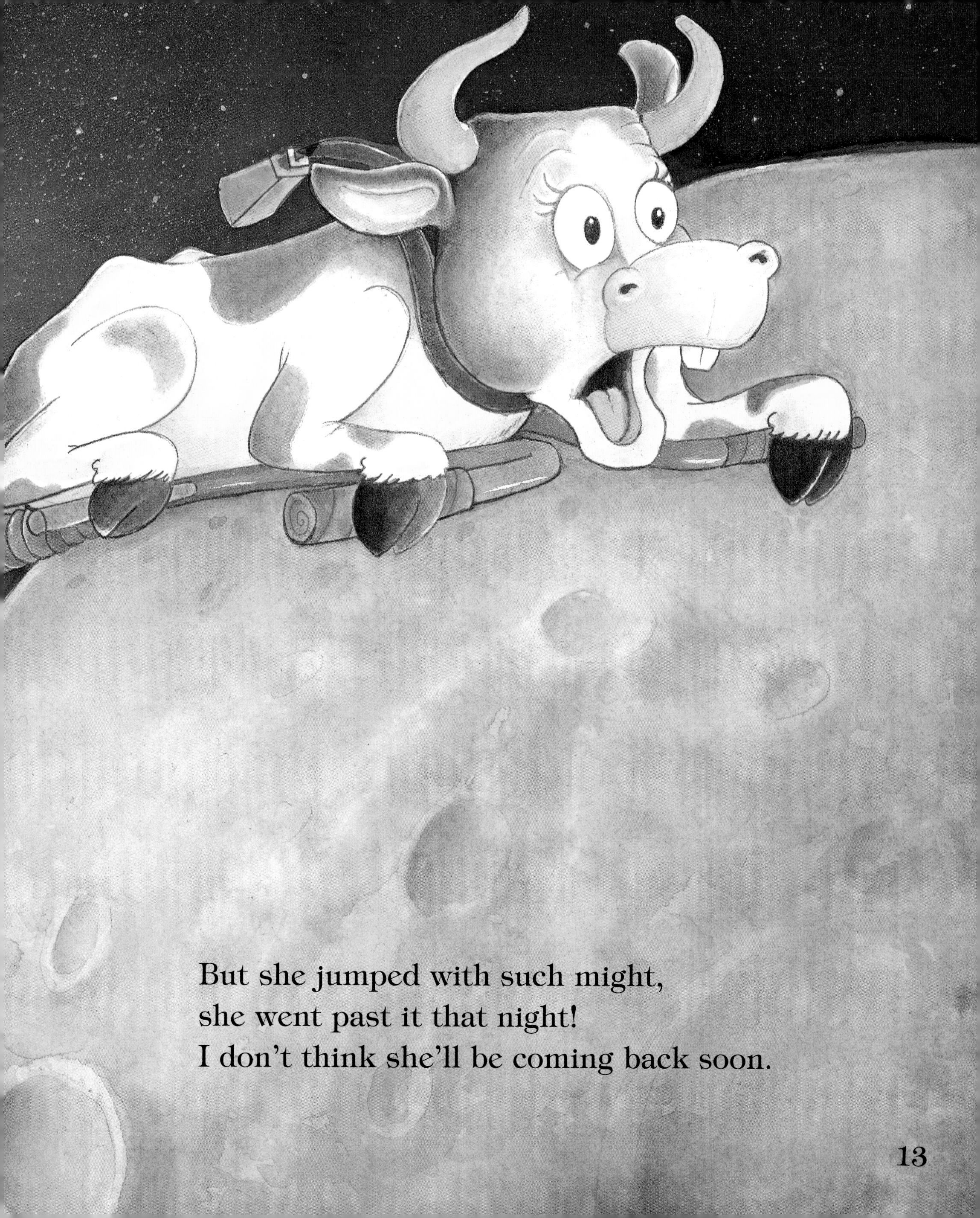

But she jumped with such might,
she went past it that night!
I don't think she'll be coming back soon.

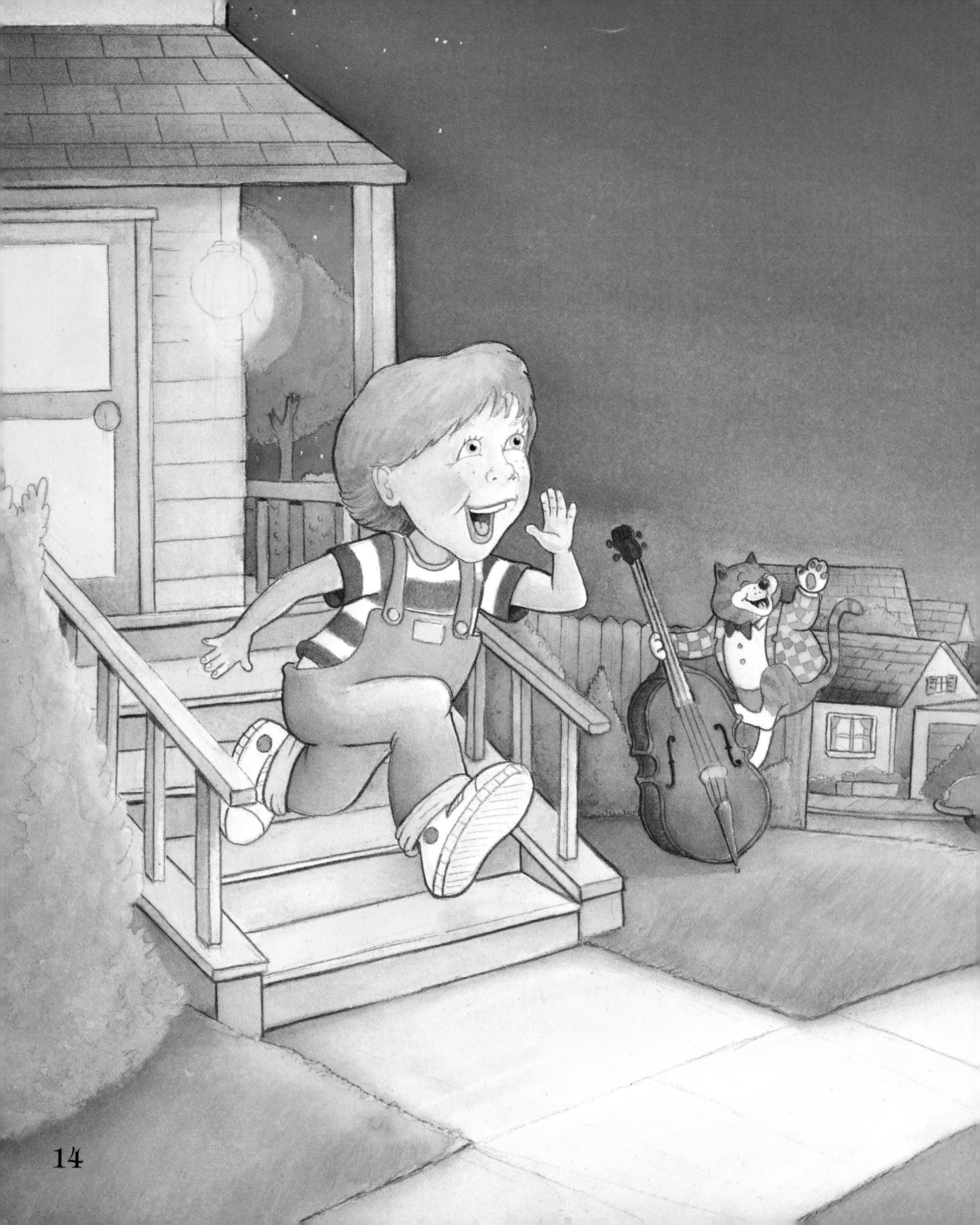

The boy, he was feeling
like running and squealing,
"Cows don't belong up in the stars!"
Though it seemed from that spot
that she traveled a lot,
the cow only made it to Mars.

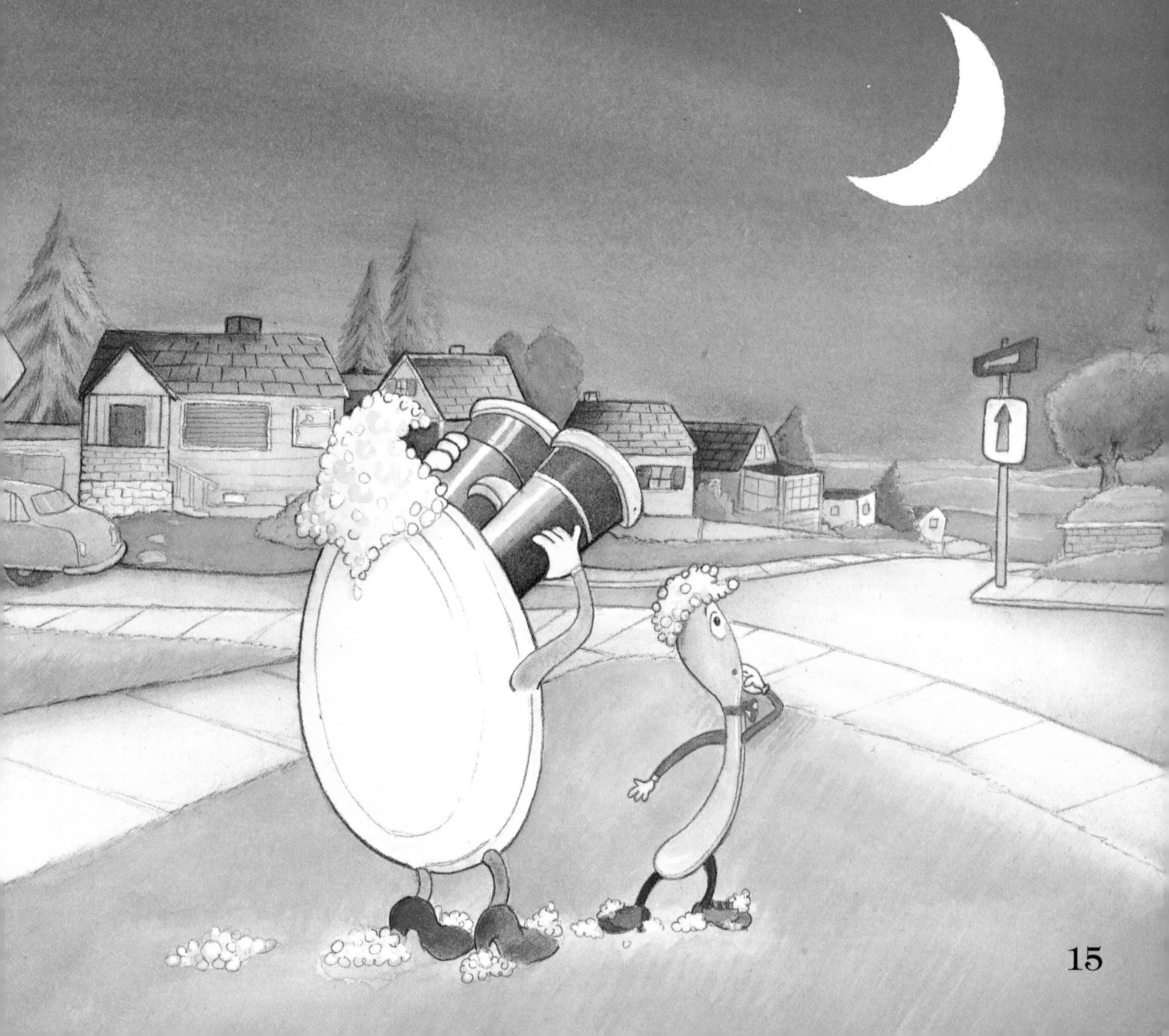

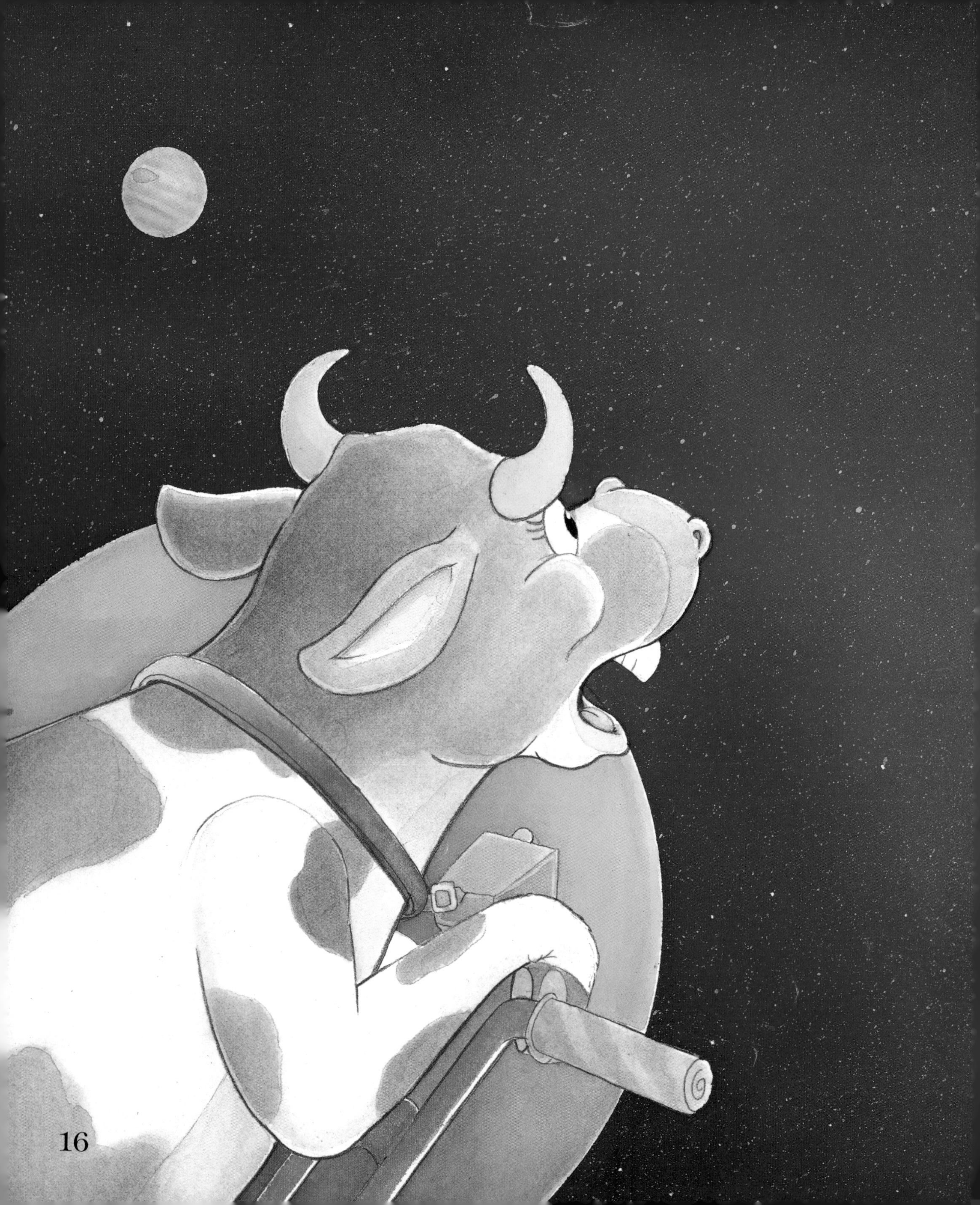

While up there in space,
the cow made a face
because she had wanted to know
what the dish and the spoon,
so far from the moon,
were doing on the planet below.

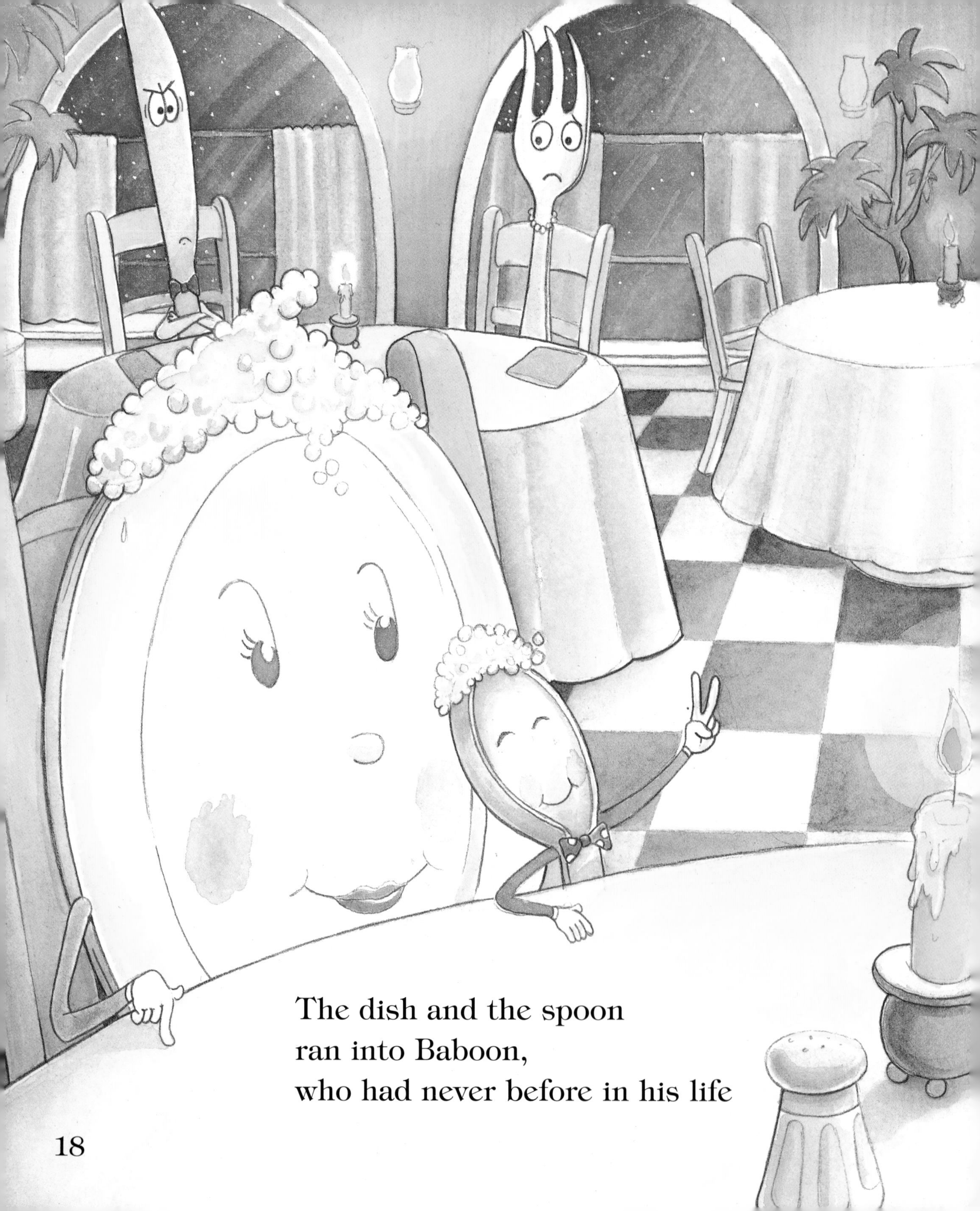

The dish and the spoon
ran into Baboon,
who had never before in his life

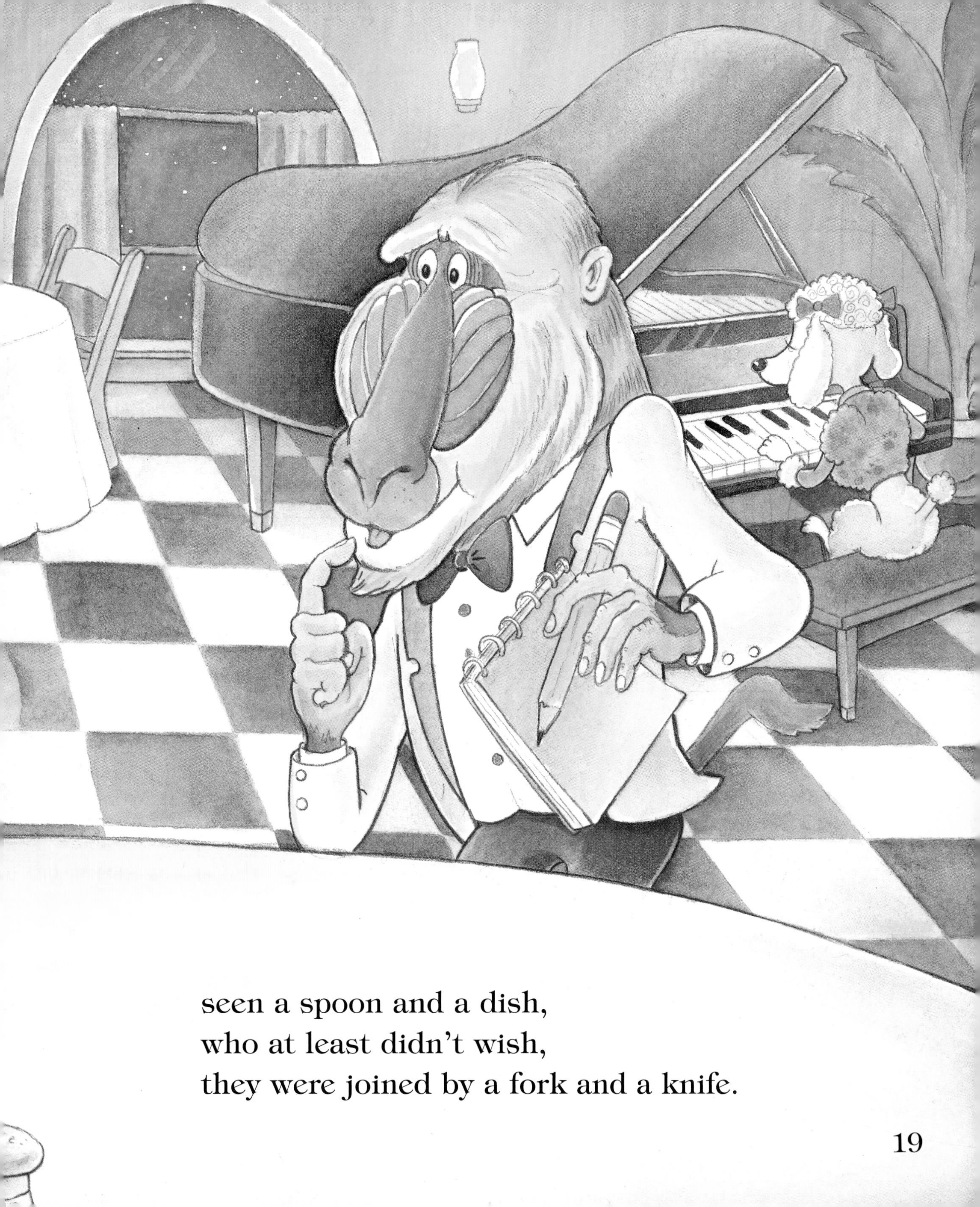

seen a spoon and a dish,
who at least didn't wish,
they were joined by a fork and a knife.

Baboon and the boy
sat and played with a toy,
as the cat danced into the room.

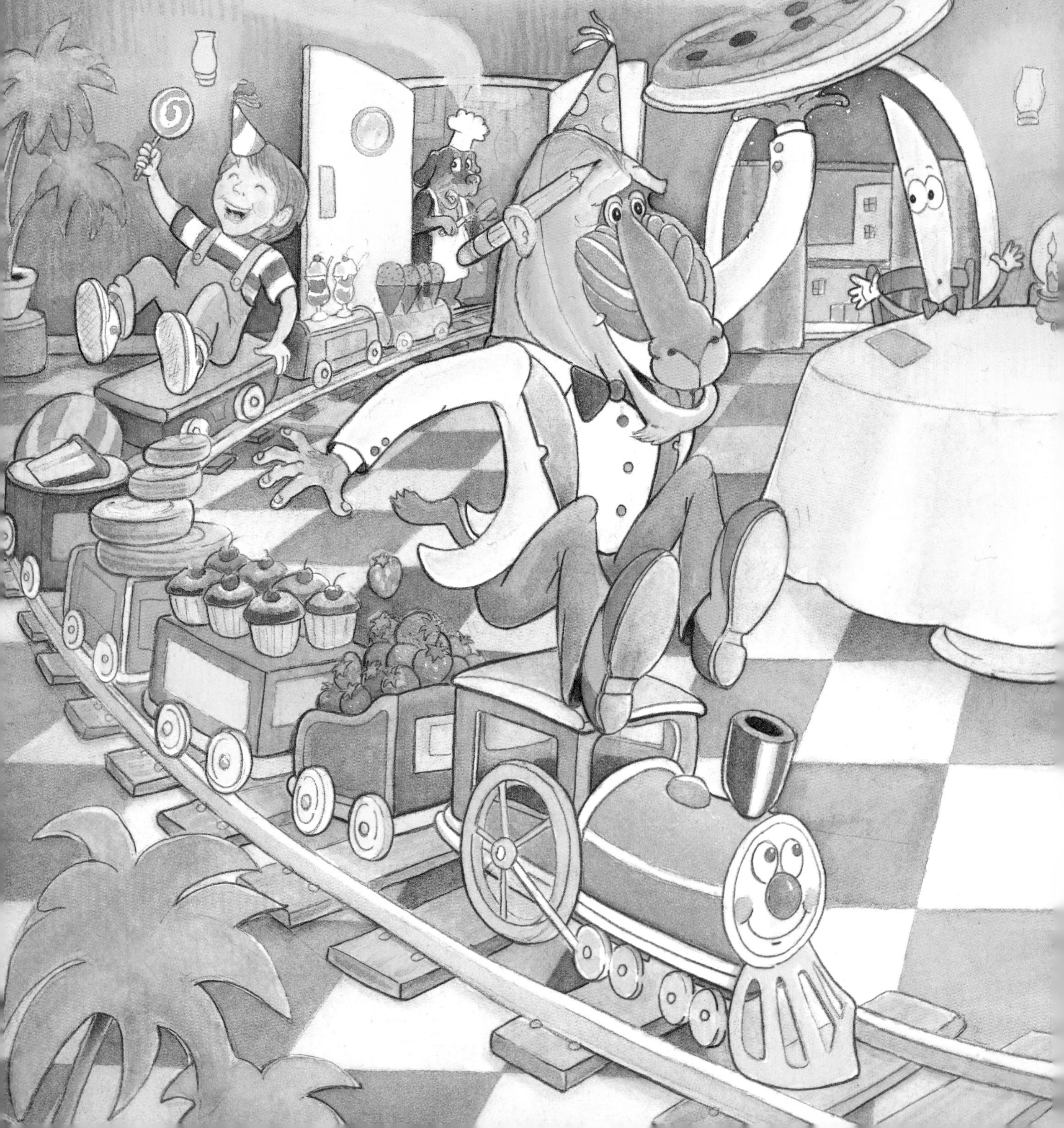

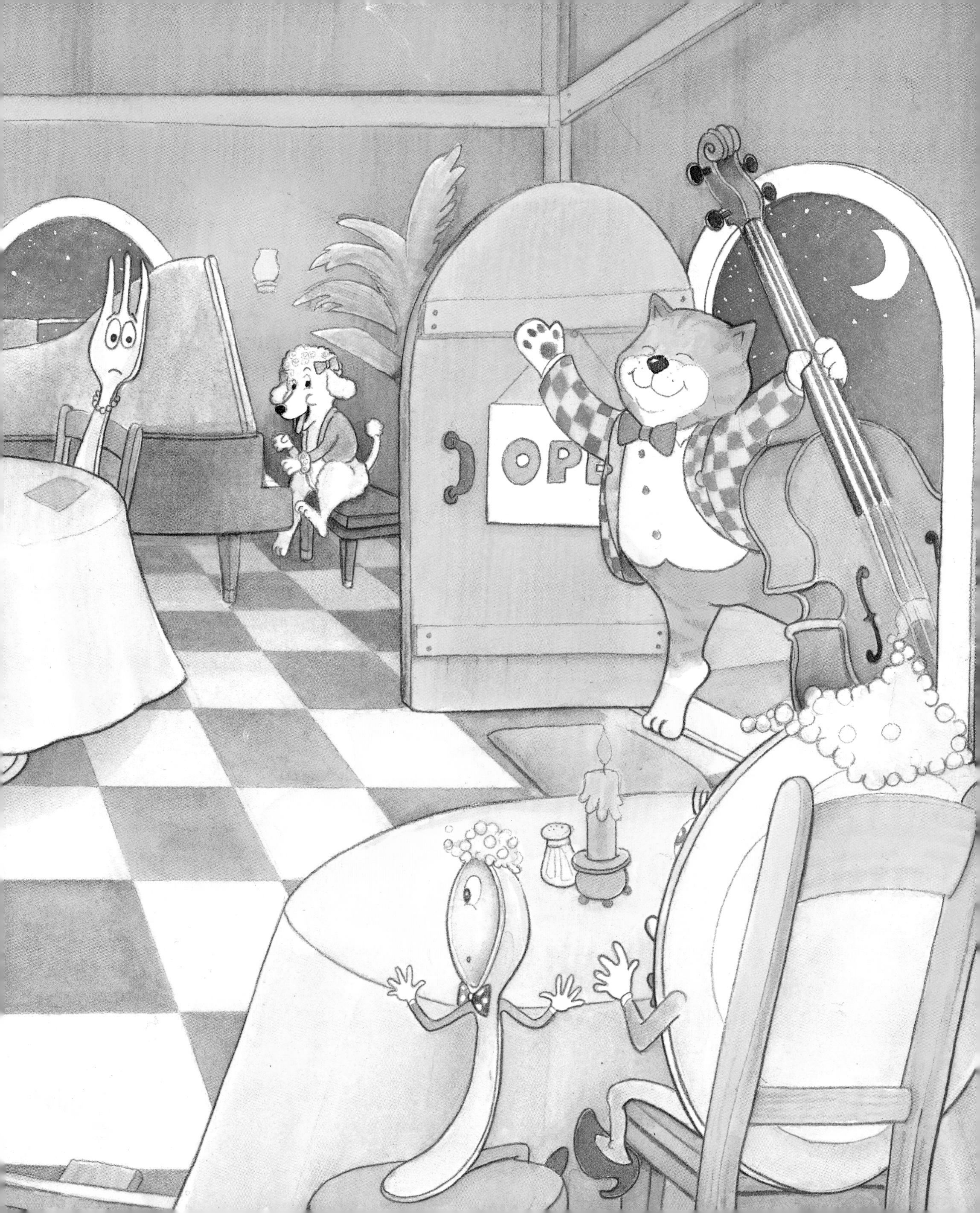
OPE

Then the boy and the cat
(who was terribly fat)
did a jig with the mop and the broom.

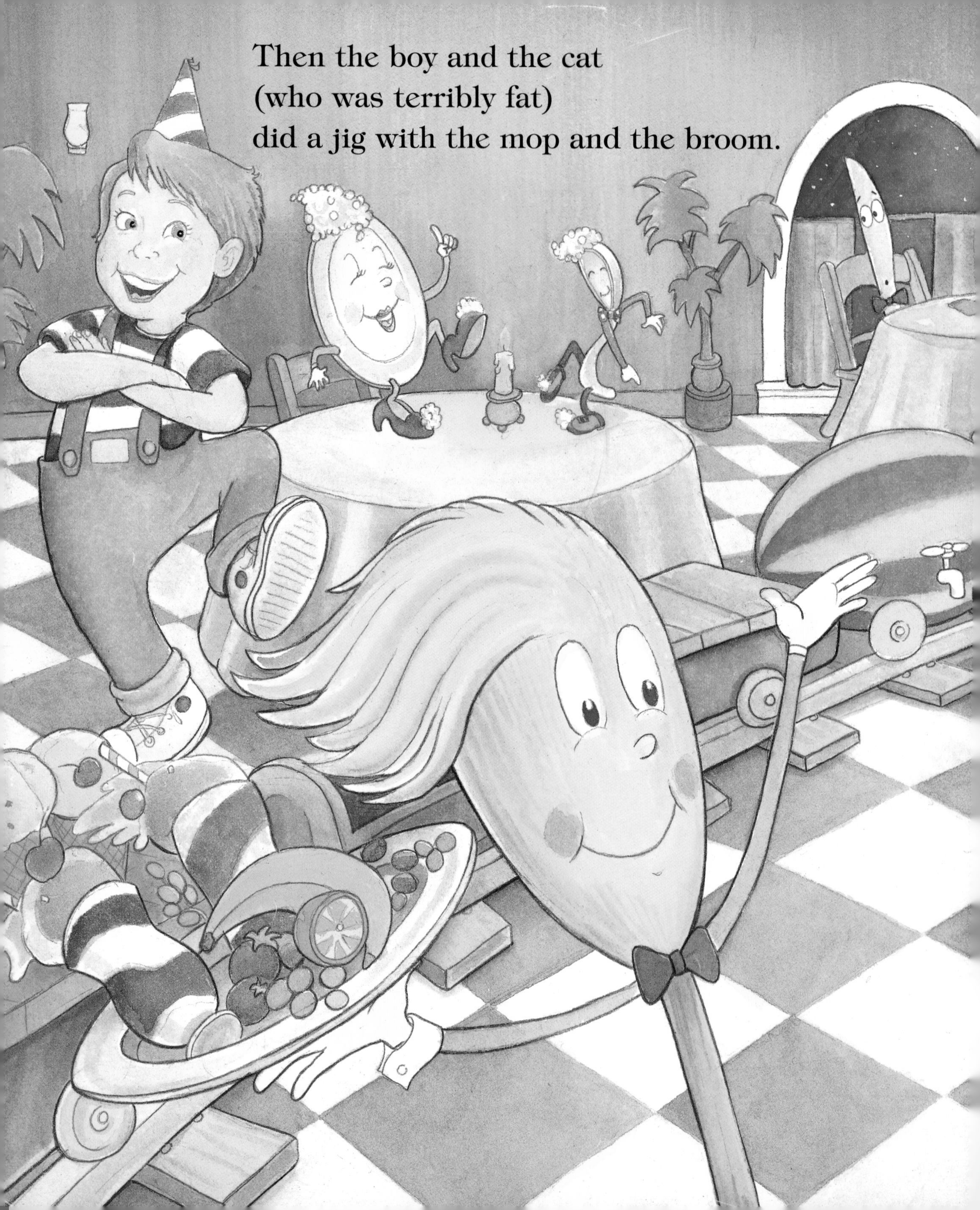

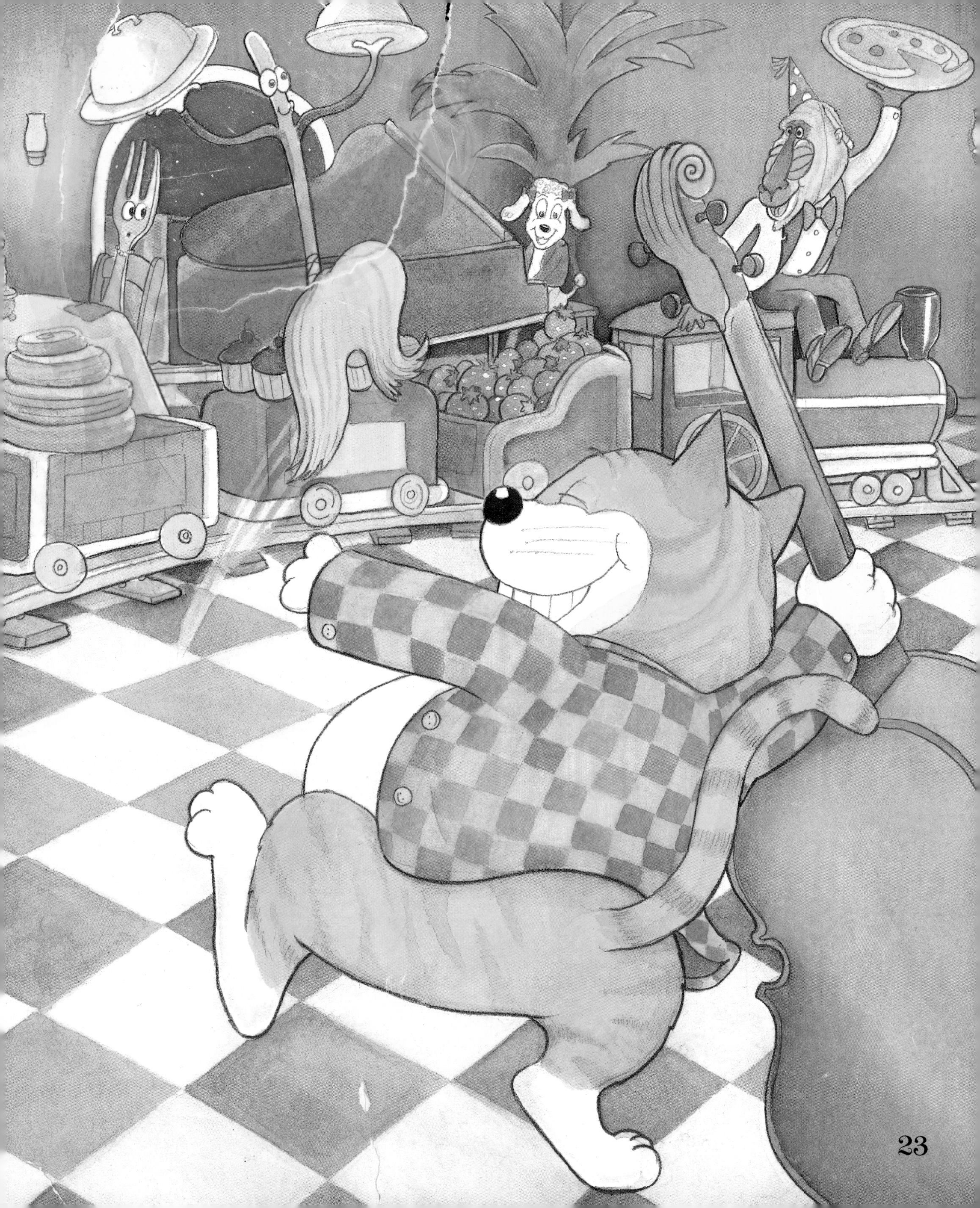

Hey, Yankee Doodle!
The cat loved the poodle;
you'd think they always would fight.

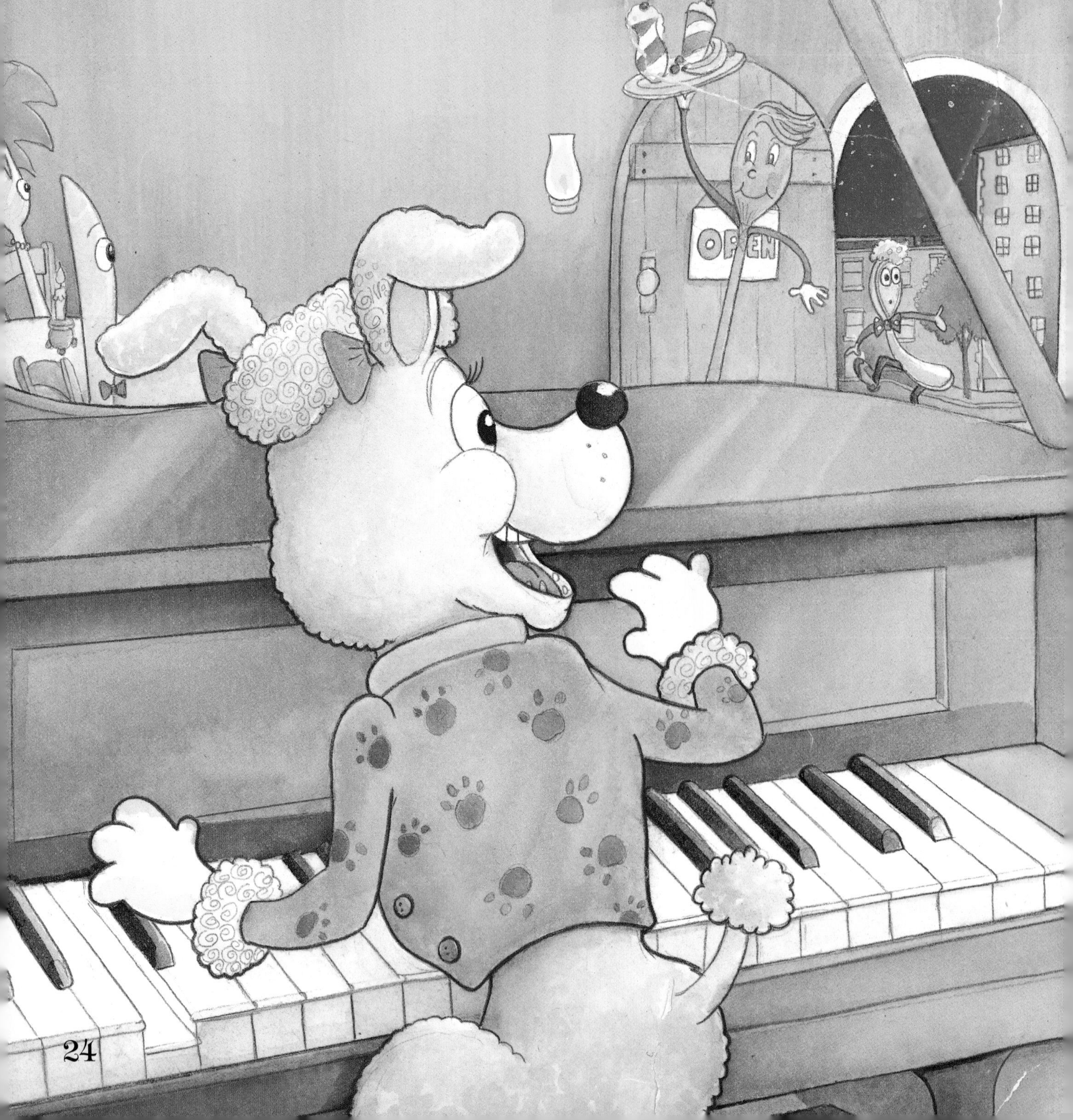
OPEN

But they loved each other
like sister and brother
and so it seemed perfectly right.

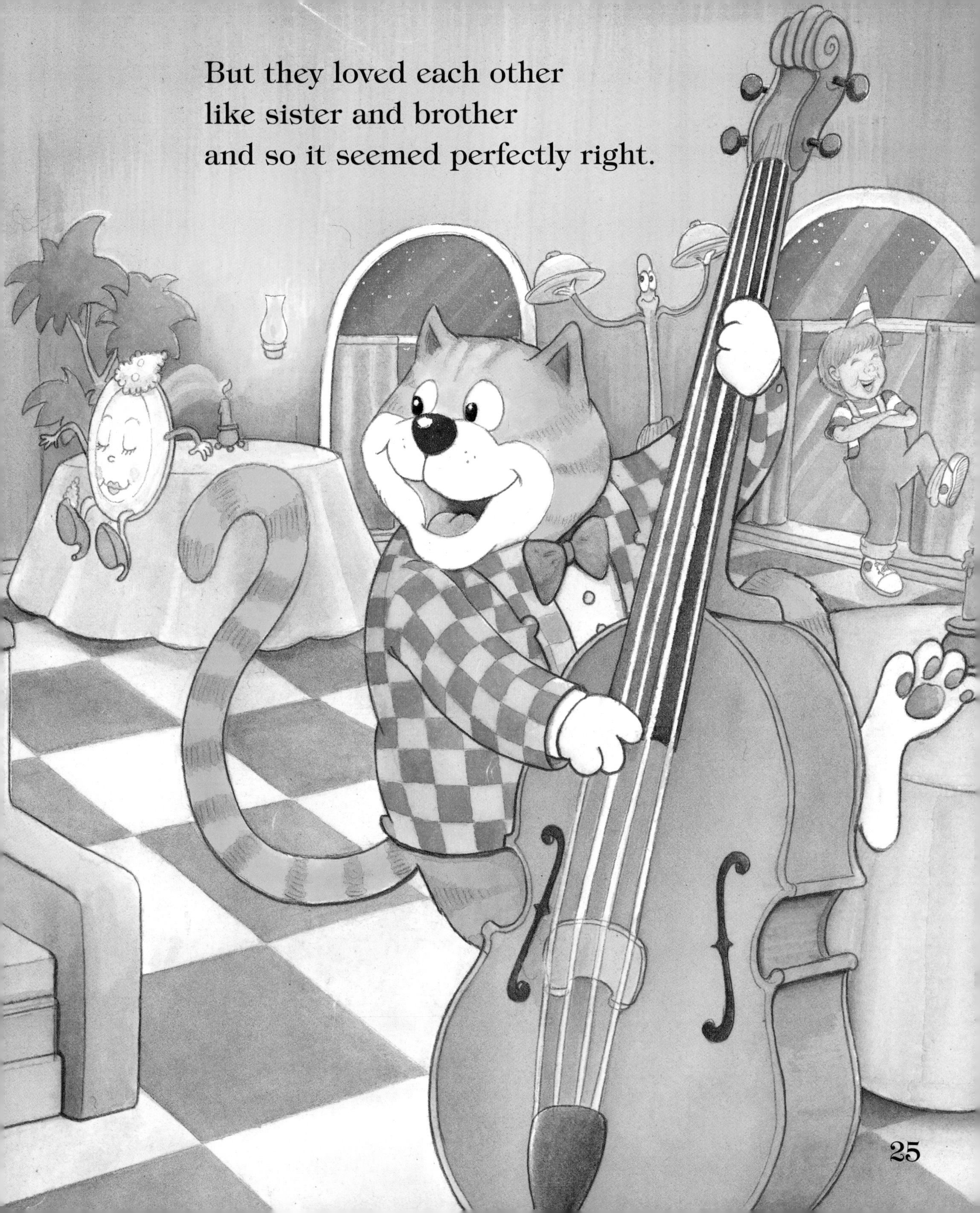

The boy and the cat
relaxed as they sat
when some dust fell down from the moon.

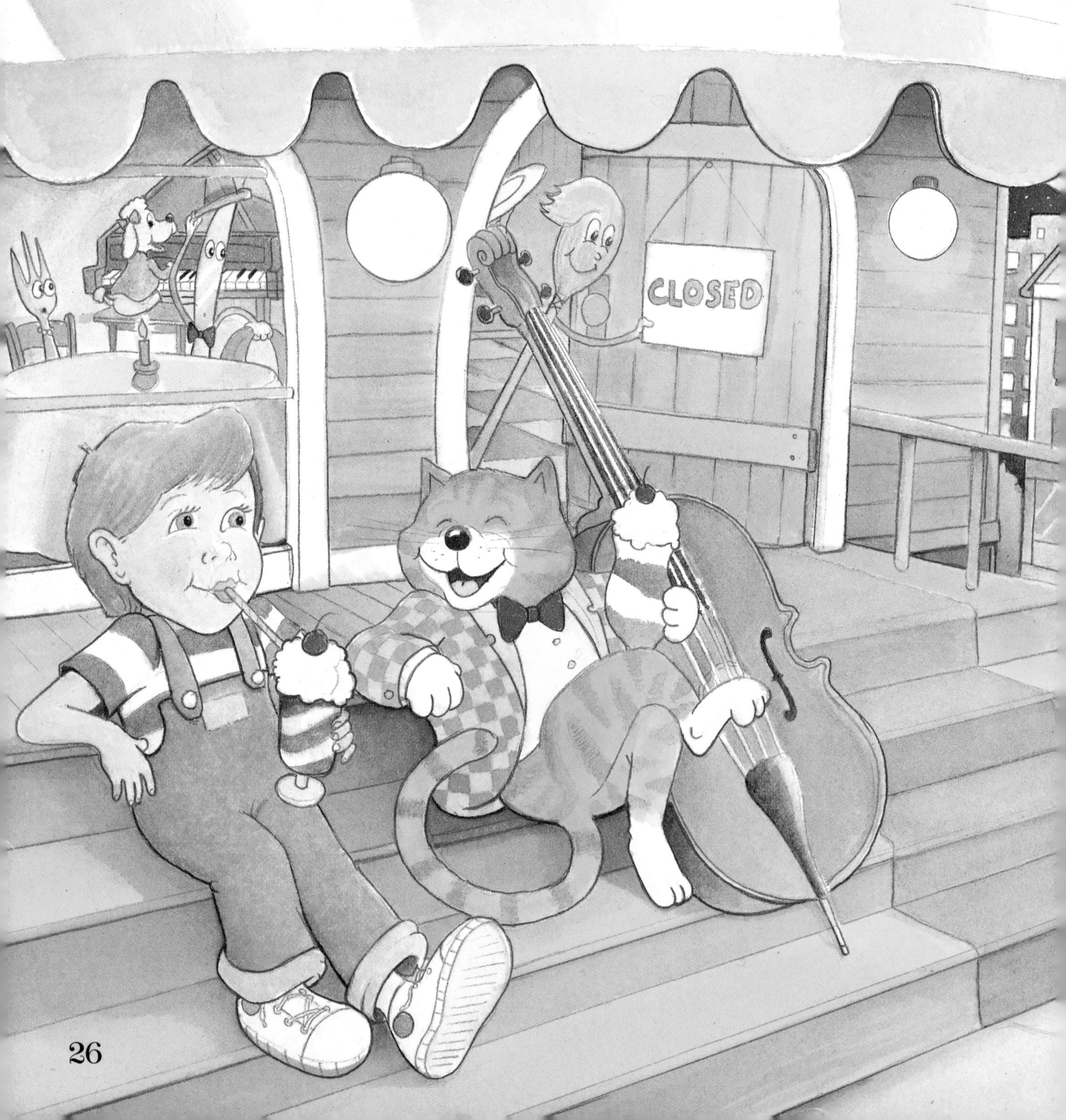
CLOSED

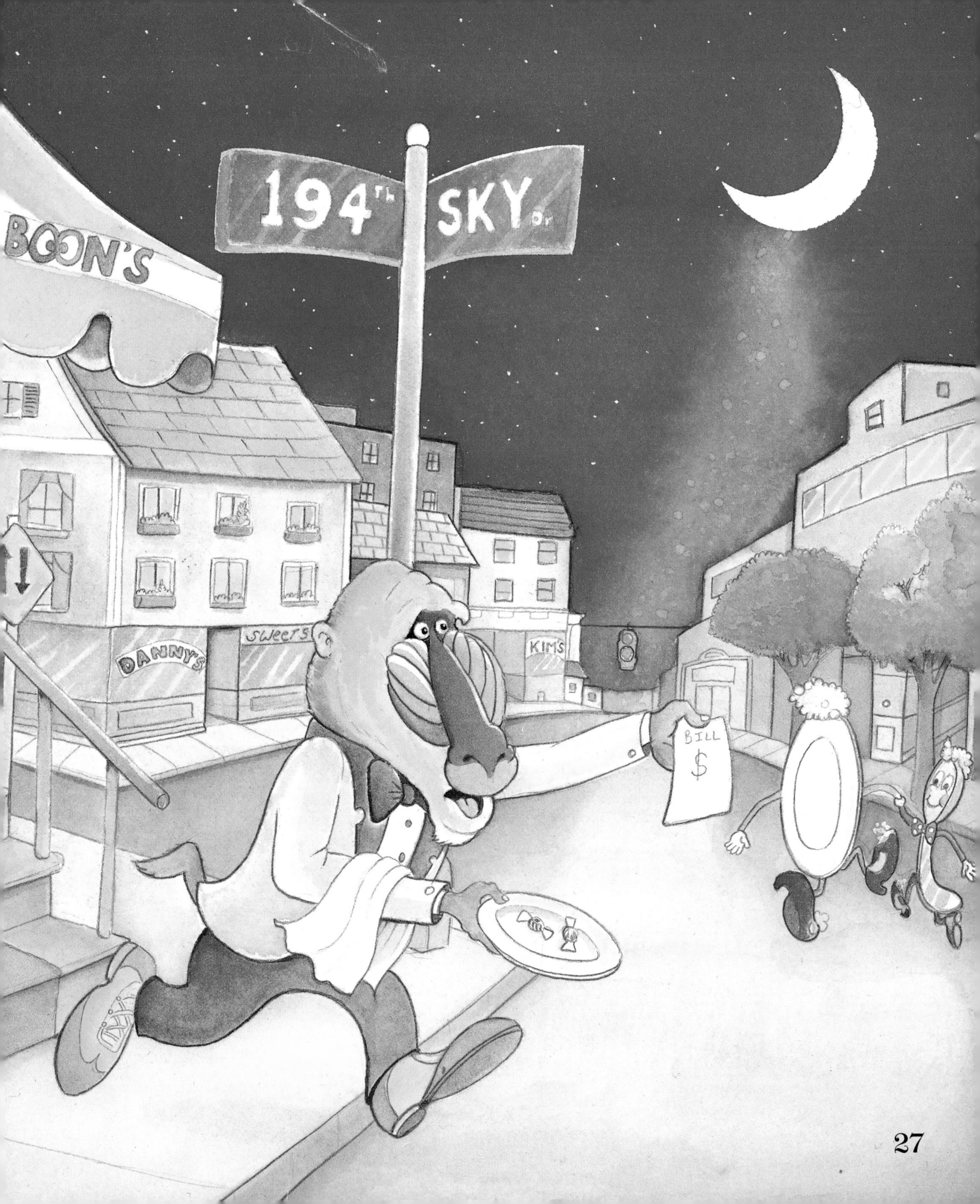
194Th
SKY Dr
BOON'S
DANNY'S
sweets
KIM'S
BILL
$

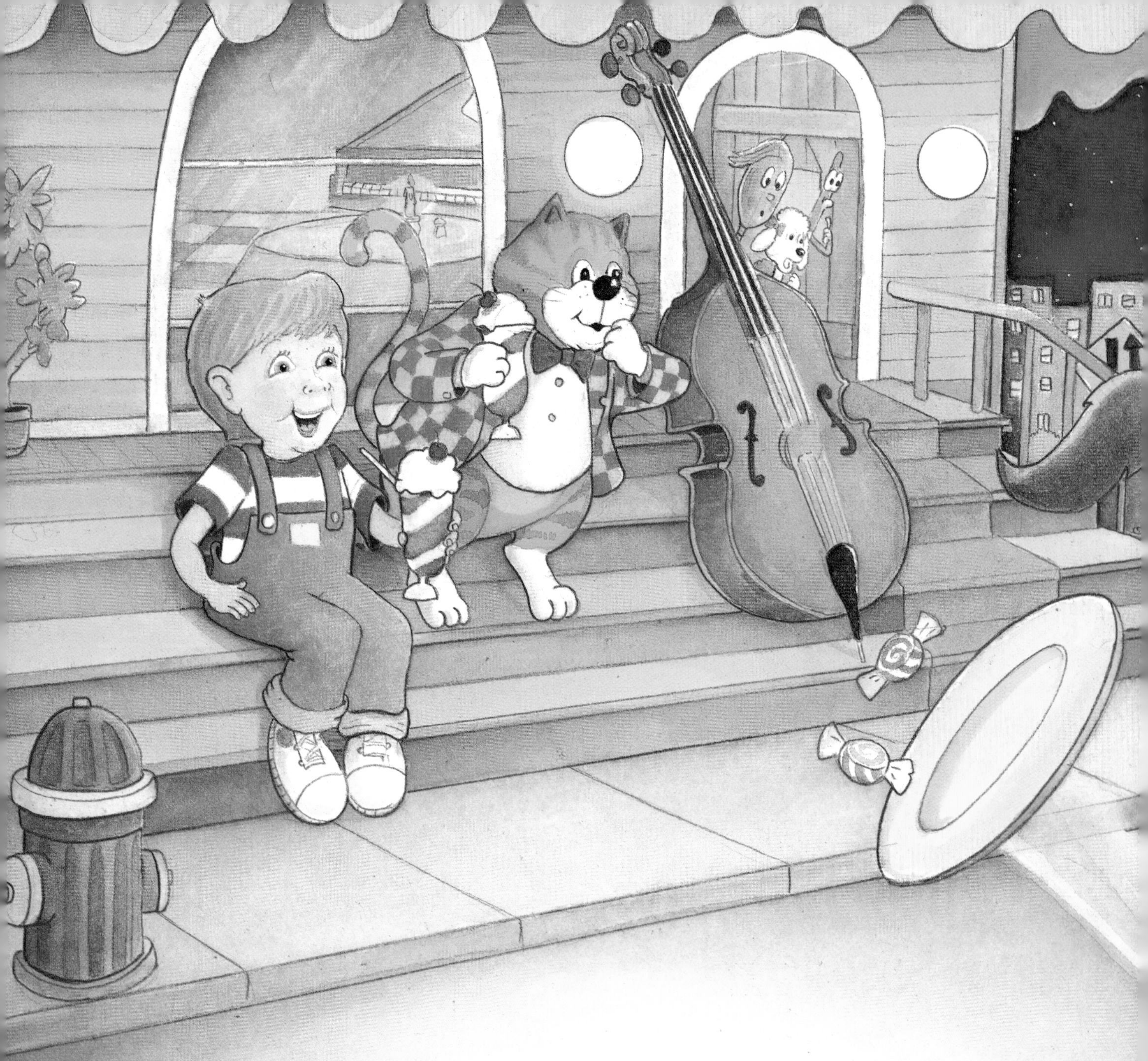

They looked up from the ground,
saw the cow floating down
and she squealed as she fell on Baboon.

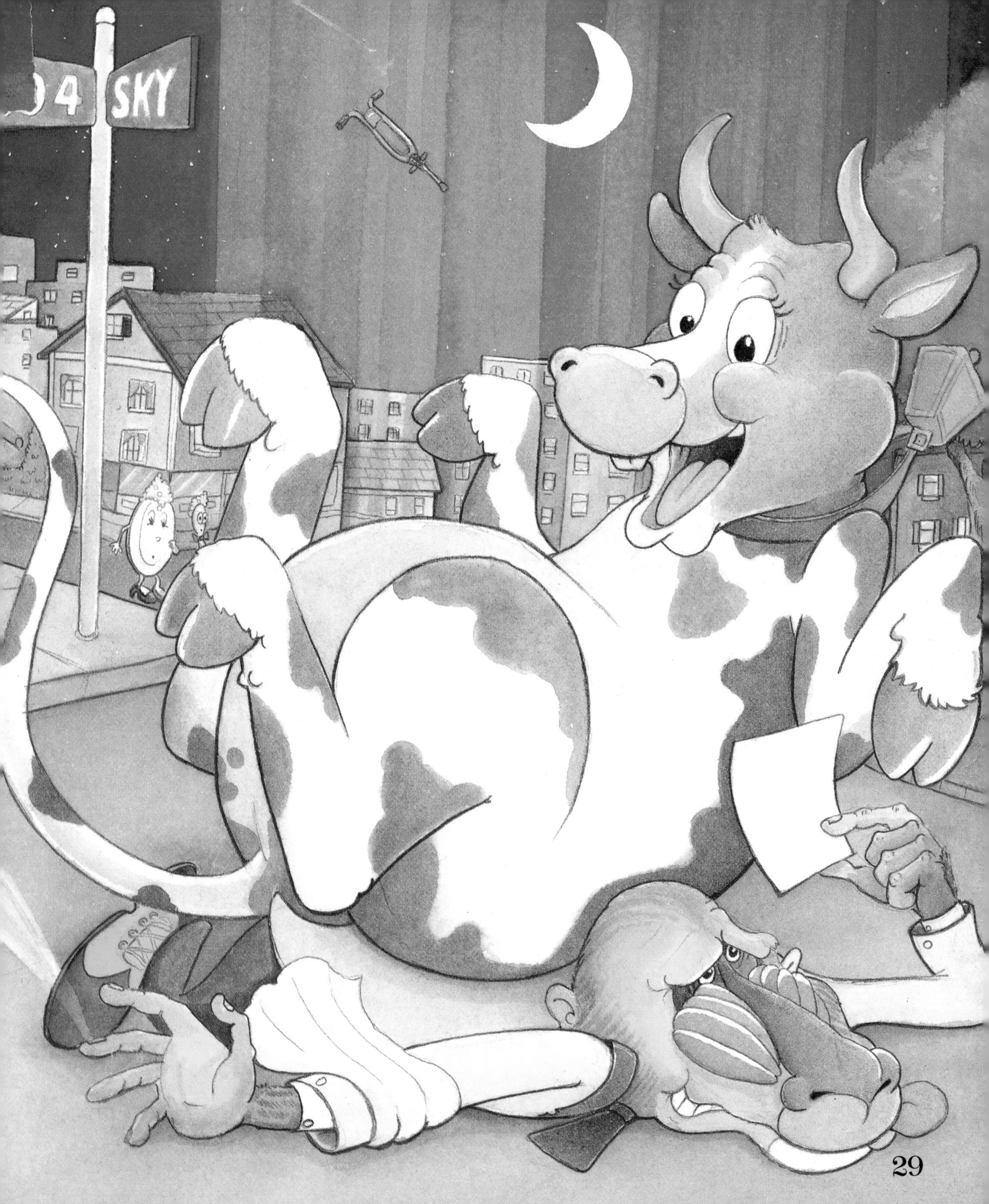

SKY

The cow and Baboon,
the dish and the spoon,
the cat and the fiddle and boy,
don't care what they play,
as long as each day
is filled with laughter and joy!

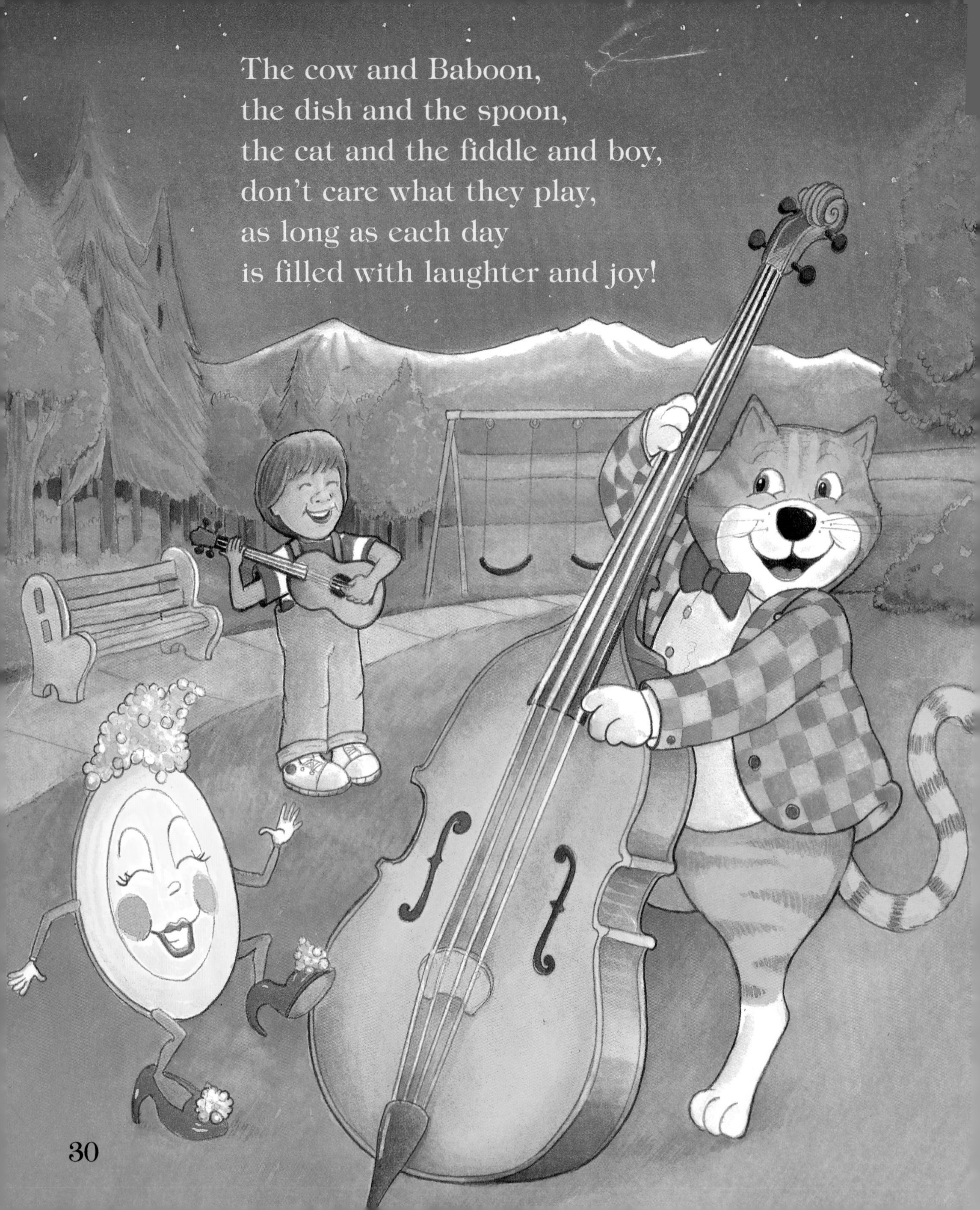

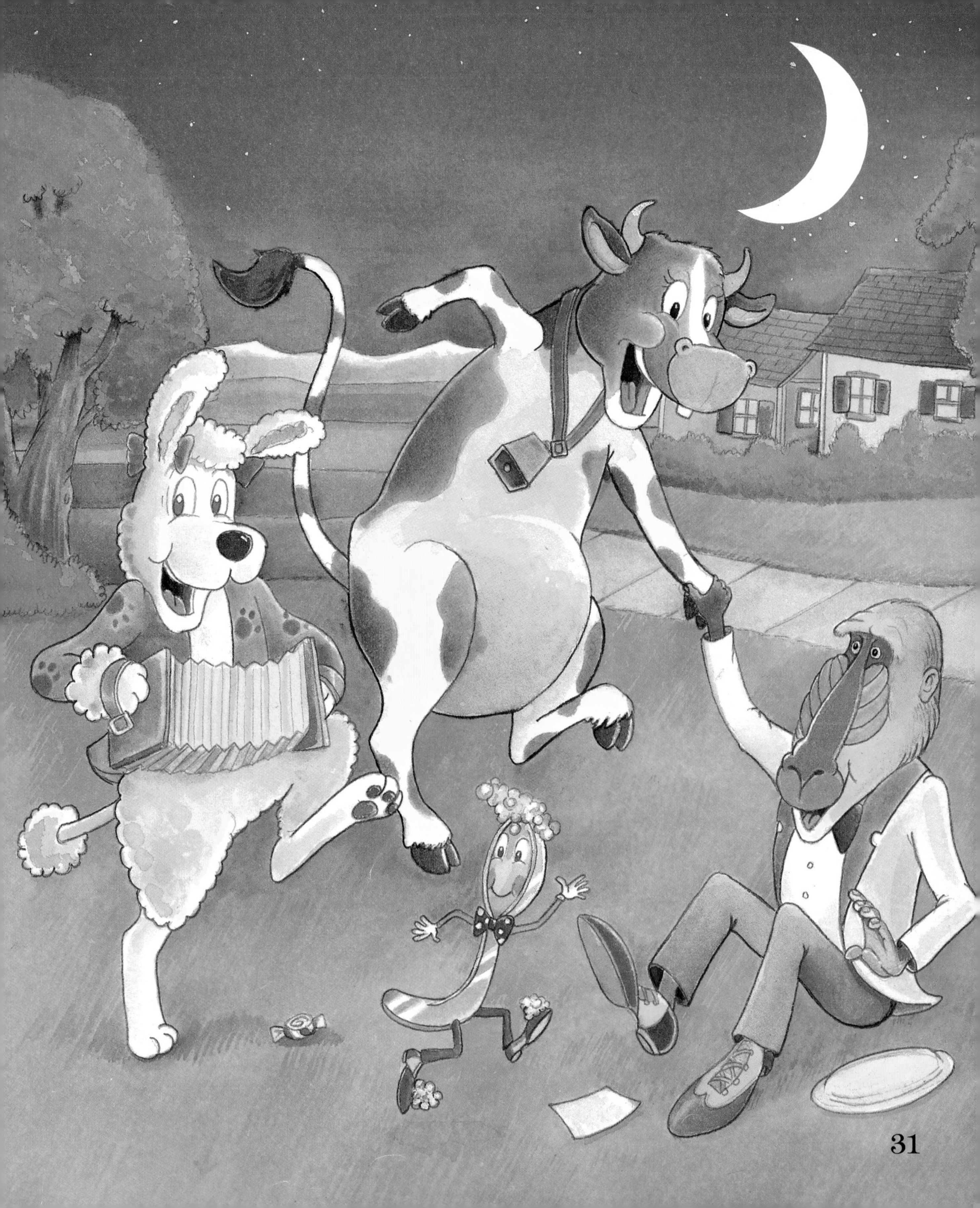

Hey, Diddle Diddle

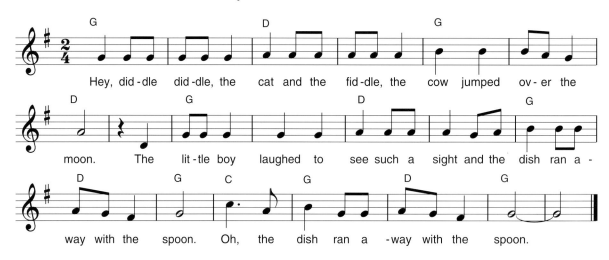

Hey, did-dle did-dle, the cat and the fid-dle, the cow jumped ov-er the moon. The lit-tle boy laughed to see such a sight and the dish ran a-way with the spoon. Oh, the dish ran a-way with the spoon.

2. The puss with the fiddle
asked his new friend a riddle:
"What's black, what's white, and brown, too?"
"Don't know," said the cow,
"I give up, tell me now."
And they laughed, "Silly cow, why it's you!"

3. The cow was out grazing
when just then—amazing!—
she suddenly leaped to the moon.
But she jumped with such might,
she went past it that night!
I don't think she'll be coming back soon.

4. The boy, he was feeling
like running and squealing,
"Cows don't belong up in the stars!"
Though it seemed from that spot
that she traveled a lot,
the cow only made it to Mars.

5. While up there in space,
the cow made a face
because she had wanted to know
what the dish and the spoon,
so far from the moon,
were doing on the planet below.

6. The dish and the spoon
ran into Baboon,
who had never before in his life
seen a spoon and a dish,
who at least didn't wish,
they were joined by a fork and a knife.

7. Baboon and the boy
sat and played with a toy,
as the cat danced into the room.
Then the boy and the cat
(who was terribly fat)
did a jig with the mop and the broom.

8. Hey, Yankee Doodle!
The cat loved the poodle;
you'd think they always would fight.
But they loved each other
like sister and brother
and so it seemed perfectly right.

9. The boy and the cat
relaxed as they sat
when some dust fell down from the moon.
They looked up from the ground,
saw the cow floating down
and she squealed as she fell on Baboon.

10. The cow and Baboon,
the dish and the spoon,
the cat and the fiddle and boy,
don't care what they play,
as long as each day
is filled up with laughter and joy!